**GULITH**
New York

Flight Through Tomorrow

Stanton A. Coblentz

ISBN: 978-1-63652-328-6

# FLIGHT THROUGH TOMORROW

STANTON A. COBLENTZ

# TABLE OF CONTENTS

# I

Nothing was further from my mind, when I discovered the "Release Drug" Relin, than the realization that it would lead me through as strange and ghastly and revealing a series of adventures as any man has ever experienced. I encountered it, in a way, as a mere by-product of my experiments; I am a chemist by profession, and as one of the staff of the Morganstern Foundation have access to some of the best equipped laboratories in America. The startling new invention—I must call it that, though I did not create it deliberately—came to me in the course of my investigations into the obscure depths of the human personality.

It has long been my theory that there is in man a psychic entity which can exist for at least brief periods apart from the body, and have perceptions which are not those of the physical senses. In accordance with these views, I had been developing various drugs, compounded of morphine and adrenalin, whose object was to shock the psychic entity loose for limited periods and so to widen the range and powers of the personality. I shall not go into the details of my researches, nor tell by what accident I succeeded better than I had hoped; the all-important fact—a fact so overwhelming that I shudder and gasp and marvel even as I tell of it—is that I did obtain a minute quantity of a drug which, by putting the body virtually in a state of suspended animation, could release the mind to travel almost at will across time and space.

Yes, across time and space!—for the drag of the physical having been stricken off, I could enter literally into infinity and eternity. But let me tell precisely what happened that night when at precisely 10:08 in the solitude of my apartment room, I swallowed half an ounce of Relin and stretched myself out on the bed, well knowing that I was taking incalculable risks, and that insanity and even death were by no means remote possibilities of the road ahead. But let that be as it may! In my opinion, there is no coward more despicable than he who will not face danger for the sake of knowledge.

My head reeled, and something seemed to buzz inside it as soon as the bitter half ounce of fluid slipped down my throat. I was barely able to reach the bed and throw myself upon it when there came a snapping as of something inside my brain ... then, for a period, blankness ... then a gradual awakening with that feeling of exhilaration one experiences only after the most blissful sleep. I opened my eyes, feeling strong and light of limb and charged with a marvelous vital energy—but, as I peered about me, my lips drew far apart in astonishment, and I am sure that I gaped like one who has seen a ghost.

Where were the familiar walls of my two-by-four room, the bureau, the book-rack, the ancient portrait of Pasteur that hung in its glass frame just above the foot of the bed? Gone! vanished as utterly as though they had never been! I was standing on a wide and windy plain, with the gale beating in my ears, and with rapid sunset-colored clouds scudding across the blood-stained west. Mingled with the wailing of the blast, there was a deep sobbing sound that struck me in successive waves, like the ululations of great multitudes of far-off mourners. And while I was wondering what this might mean and felt a prickling of horror along my spine, the first of the portents swept across the sky. I say "portents," for I do not know by what other term to describe the apparitions; high in the heavens, certainly at an altitude of many miles, the flaming thing swept across my view, comet-shaped and stretching over at least ten degrees of arc, swift as a meteor, brilliantly flesh-red, sputtering sparks like an anvil, and leaving behind it a long ruddy trail that only slowly faded out amid the darkening skies.

It must have been a full minute after its disappearance before the hissing of its flight came to my ears—a hissing so sharp, so nastily insistent that it reached me even above the noise of the wind. And more than another minute had passed before the earth beneath me was wrenched and jarred as if by an earthquake and the most thunderous detonations I had ever heard burst over me in a prolonged series.

Let me emphasize that none of this had the quality of a dream; it was clear-cut, as vivid as anything I had ever experienced; my mind worked with an unusual precision and clarity, and not even a fleeting doubt came to me of the reality of my observations. "This is some sort of bombing attack," I remember reflecting, "some assault of super-monsters of the skies, perfected by a super science." And I did not have to be told the fact; I knew, as by an all-illuminating inner knowledge, that I had voyaged into the future.

Even as this realization came to me, I made another flight—and one that was in space more than in time. It did not surprise me, but I took it as the most natural thing in the world when I seemed to rise and go floating away through the air. It was still sunset-time, but I could see clearly enough as I went drifting at a height of several hundred yards above a vast desolated space near the junction of two rivers. Perhaps, however, "desolated" is not the word I should use; I should say, rather, "shattered, pulverized, obliterated," for a scene of more utter and hopeless ruin I have never seen nor imagined. Over an area of many square miles, there was nothing but heaps and mounds of broken stone, charred and crumbling brick, fire-scarred timbers, and huge contorted masses of rusting steel like the decaying bones of superhuman monsters. From the great height and extent of the piles of debris, and from the occasional sight of the splintered cornice of a roof or of some battered window-frame or door, I knew that this had once been a city, one of the world's greatest; but no other recognizable feature remained amid the gray masses of ruins, and the very streets and avenues had been erased. But here and there a tremendous crater, three hundred feet across and a hundred to a hundred and fifty feet deep, indicated the source of the destruction.

As if to reinforce the dread idea that had taken possession of my brain, one of the comet-like red prodigies went streaking across the sky even as I gazed down at the dead city; and I knew—as clearly as if I had seen the whole spectacle with my own eyes—that the missile had sprung from a source hundreds or thousands of miles away, possibly across the ocean; and that, laden with scores of tons of explosives, it had been hurled with unerring mechanical accuracy upon its mission of annihilation.

Then I seemed to float over vast distances of that sunset-tinted land, and saw great craters in the fields, and villages shot to ribbons, and farms abandoned; and the wild dogs fought for the wild cattle; and thistles grew deep on acres where wheat had been planted, and weeds sprouted thickly in the orchards, and blight and mildew competed for the crops. But though here and there I could see a dugout, with traces of fire and abandoned tools flung about at random, nowhere in all that dismal world did I observe a living man.

After a time I returned to a place near the ruined city by the two rivers; and in the rocky palisades above one of the streams, I made out some small circular holes barely large enough to admit a man. And, borne onward by some impulse of curiosity and despair, I entered one of these holes, and went downward, far downward into the dim recesses. And now for the first time, at a depth of hundreds of yards, I did at last encounter living men. My first thought was that I had gone back to the day of the cave-man, for a cave-like hollow had been scooped out in the solid rock. It was true that the few hundreds of people huddled together there had the dress and looks of moderns; it was true, also, that the gloom was lighted for them by electric bulbs, and that electric radiators kept them warm; yet Dante himself, in painting the ninth circle of his Inferno, could not have imagined a drearier and more despondent group than these that slouched and drooped and muttered in that cavernous recess, seated with their heads fallen low upon their knees, or moodily pacing back and forth like captives who can hope for no escape. "Here at least we will be safe from the sky marauders," I heard one of them muttering. Yet I could not help wondering what the mere safety of the body could mean when all the glories of man's civilization were annihilated.

# II

There came a whirring in my head, and another blank interval; and when I regained my senses I knew that another period of time had passed, possibly months or even years. I stood on the palisade above the river, near the entrance of the caves; and the sun was bright above me; but there was no brightness in the men and women that trailed out of a small circular hole in the ground. Drab as dock-rats, and pasty pale of countenance as hospital inmates, and with bent backs and dirty, tattered clothes and a mouse-like nosing manner, they emerged with the wariness of hunted refugees; and they flung up their hands with low cries to shield them from the brilliance of the sun, to which they were evidently unaccustomed. From the packs on their backs and the bundles in their hands, I knew that they were emerging from their subterranean refuge, to try to begin a new life in the ravaged world above; and my heart went out to them, for I saw that, few as they were—not more than fifty in all—they were the sole survivors of a once-populous region, and would have a bitter fight to wage in the man-made wilderness that had been a world metropolis.

But as they roamed above through the waste of ash and rubble, and as they wandered abroad where the fields had been and saw how every brush and tree had been seared from the earth or poisoned by chemical brews, I knew that their fight was not merely a bitter one—it was hopeless. And I heard them muttering among themselves, "We have not even any tools!", and again, "We have no fuel left for the great machines!" ... For they had lived in a highly mechanical world, and the technicians who alone understood the workings of that world had all been destroyed, and the sources of power had all been cut off—and power was the food without which they could not long survive.

Unable to endure their haggard, hangdog looks and grim, despondent eyes, I went wandering far away, over the length and breadth of many lands. And nowhere did I see a factory that had not been hammered to dust, nor a village that had not been unroofed or burnt, nor a farm where the workers went humming on their merry, toilsome way. Yet here and there I did observe little knots of survivors. Sometimes they were half-clad groups, lean and ferocious as famished wolves, who roamed the houseless countryside with stones and clubs, hunting the wild birds and hares, or making meager meals from bark and roots. Sometimes three or four men, with the frenzied eyes and hysterical shrieks and shouts of maniacs, would emerge from a brush hut by a river flat. Sometimes little bands of men and women, in a dazed aimless way, would go wandering about a huge jagged hole in the ground, where their homes and their loved ones lay buried. I came upon solitary refugees high up on the scarred mountain slopes, with nothing but a staff to lean upon and a deer-skin to keep them warm. I saw more than one twisted form lying motionless at the foot of a precipice. I witnessed a battle between two half-crazed, ravenous bands, with murder, and cannibalism, and horrors too grisly to report. I observed brave men resolutely trying to till the soil, whose productive powers had been ruined by a poison spray from the sky; and I noted some who, though the fields remained fertile enough, had not the seed to plant; and others who had not the tools with which to plow and reap.

And some who, with great labor, managed to produce enough for three or four mouths, had twenty or thirty to feed; and where the three or four might have lived, the twenty or thirty perished.

Then, with a great sadness, I knew that man, having become civilized, cannot make himself into a savage again. He has come to depend upon science for his sustenance, and when he himself has destroyed the means of employing that science, he is as a babe without milk. And it is not necessary to destroy all men in order to exterminate mankind; one need only take from him the prop of his mechanical inventions.

**III**

Again there came a blankness, and I passed over a stretch of time, perhaps over years or even decades. And I had wandered far in space, to an island somewhere on a sunny sea; and there once more I heard the sound of voices. And somehow, through some deeper sense, I knew that these were the voices of the only men left anywhere on the whole wide planet. And I looked down on them, and saw that they were but few, no more than a dozen men and women in all, with three or four children among them. But their faces, unlike those which I had seen before, were not haggard and seamed, nor avid like those of hunting beasts, nor distorted by fury or famine. Their brows were broad and noble, and their eyes shone with the sweetness of great thoughts, and their smiles were as unuttered music; and when they glanced at me with their clear, level gaze, I knew that they were such beings as poets had pictured as dwellers in a far tomorrow. And I did not feel sad, though I could not forget that they were the only things in human form that one could find on all earth's shores, and though I knew that they were too few to perpetuate their kind for long. Somehow I felt some vast benevolent spirit in control, that these most perfect specimens of our race should endure when all the wreckers had vanished.

As I watched, I saw the people all turning their eyes to an eastern mountain, whose summit still trailed the golden of the dawn-clouds. And from above the peak a great illuminated sphere, like a chariot of light, miraculously came floating down; and the blaze was such that I could hardly bear to look at it. And exclamations of wonder and joy came from the people's throats; and I too cried out in joy and wonder as the radiant globe descended, and as it alighted on the plain before us, casting a sunlike aura over everything in sight. Then through the sides of the enormous ball—I would not say, through the door, for nothing of the kind was visible—a glorious being emerged, followed by several of his kind. He was shaped like a man, and was no taller than a man, and yet there was that about him which said that he was greater than a man, for light seemed to pour from every cell of his body, and a golden halo was about his head, and his eyes shot forth golden beams so intense and so magnetic that, once having observed them, I could hardly take my gaze away.

With slow steps he advanced, motioning the people to him; and they drew near, and flung themselves before him on the ground, and cried out in adoration. And I too threw myself to earth, in worship of this superhuman creature; and I heard the words he spoke, and with some deeper sense I translated them, though they were not uttered in any language I knew:

"Out of the stars we come, O men! and back to the stars we shall go, that the best of your race may be transplanted there, and survive through means known to us, and again be populous and great. Through the immense evil within the breasts of your kind, you have been purged and all but annihilated; but the good within your race has also been mighty, and can never be expunged; and that good has called through you surviving few to us your guardians, that we may take you to another planet, and replenish you there, and teach you that lore of love and truth and beauty which the blind members of your species have neglected here while they unfitted the earth for human habitation."

So speaking, the radiant one motioned to the people, who arose, and followed him inside the great sphere of light; and when they had all entered, it slowly began to ascend, and slowly dwindled and disappeared against the morning skies. And now, I knew, there was no longer a man left anywhere on earth; yet as I gazed at the deserted shore, the empty beach and the bare mountainside, a sense of supreme satisfaction came over me, as though I knew that in the end, after fire and agony and degradation, all was eternally well.

That sense of supreme satisfaction remained with me when, after still another blank interval, I opened my eyes as from a deep slumber, and stared at the familiar book-rack, the bureau, the mottled paper walls of my own room. The clock on the little table at my side indicated the hour of 10:09—in other words, all that had happened had occupied the space of one minute! Yet I know as surely as I know that I write these words—that the Release Drug had freed my spirit to range over thousands of miles of space, and that I have looked on people and events which no other eye will view for scores, hundreds or even thousands of years to come.

# TRANSCRIBER'S NOTE:

This etext was produced from *Fantasy Book* Vol. 1 number 1 (1947). Extensive research did not uncover any evidence that the U.S. copyright on this publication was renewed. Minor spelling and typographical errors have been corrected without note.